Possible Friend

VIOLET MACKEREL'S

Possible Friend

Anna Branford

illustrated by
Elanna Allen

Atheneum Books for Young Readers
New York   London   Toronto   Sydney   New Delhi

Atheneum Books for Young Readers

An imprint of Simon & Schuster Children's Publishing Division

1230 Avenue of the Americas, New York, New York 10020

ATHENEUM BOOKS FOR YOUNG READERS is a registered trademark of Simon & Schuster, Inc.

Atheneum logo is a trademark of Simon & Schuster, Inc.

For information about special discounts for bulk purchases, please contact Simon & Schuster Special Sales at 1-866-506-1949 or business@simonandschuster.com.

The Simon & Schuster Speakers Bureau can bring authors to your live event. For more information or to book an event, contact the Simon & Schuster Speakers Bureau at 1-866-248-3049 or visit our website at www.simonspeakers.com.

Also available in an Atheneum Books for Young Readers hardcover edition.

Book design by Lauren Rille

The text for this book is set in Excelsior.

The illustrations for this book are rendered in pencil with digital ink.

Manufactured in the United States of America

1014 MTN

10 9 8 7 6 5 4 3 2

Library of Congress Cataloging-in-Publication Data

Branford, Anna.

Violet Mackerel's possible friend / Anna Branford ; illustrated by Elanna Allen.

p.   cm.

Summary: After moving to a new neighborhood, a girl who is both a worrier and a problem solver meets a possible very good friend next door.

ISBN 978-1-4424-9455-8 (hardcover)

ISBN 978-1-4424-9456-5 (paperback)

ISBN 978-1-4424-9457-2 (eBook)

[1. Friendship—Fiction. 2. Worry—Fiction. 3. Moving, Household—Fiction. 4. Family life—Fiction.] I. Allen, Elanna, ill. II. Title.

PZ7.B737384Vhq 2014

[Fic]—dc23 2013013568

For Holly, my niece
—A. B.

For my brand-new apple dumpling
—E. A.

Possible Friend

1 The Garden Fence

Violet Mackerel is exploring her new home. Her family has only just moved in, so she is discovering interesting things all the time.

Her first discovery in the new garden is an ants' nest. Hundreds of ants crawl in

and out, sometimes carrying things that are bigger than they are. Her next good discovery is a ring of small brown mushrooms growing in a damp spot. They look like tiny umbrellas. But the most interesting discovery for the whole morning is something that actually looks very ordinary at first. It is a brown knot in the pale wooden fence.

The knot is a dark circle with a ring around it. Violet presses it like a button to see if something happens, but she doesn't really expect that anything will. It moves. She presses a little harder and it moves a bit more. She presses harder still, and suddenly it pops right through the fence and falls out the other side.

Violet's heart does a worried little jump. She looks around to see if anyone has seen her accidentally making a hole in the fence, but everyone is much too busy to notice. Mama and Violet's brother,

Dylan, are still moving furniture, trying to find the right places for it all to fit. Mama's new husband, Vincent, is filling in cracks in the new bathroom's ceiling. Violet's sister, Nicola, is trying to find the channels on the television by reading some

instructions and pressing all different buttons on the remote. No one has seen Violet making the hole. Perhaps, Violet thinks, no one will guess it was her.

One cheering thought is that she now has a good way of peeking into the garden next door. Mama says she thinks a girl lives there who is about Violet's age. Violet doesn't have any friends near the new house, and she would quite like to make one. But making a new friend can be tricky, especially if the friend you would like to make is someone you have never met or even seen before.

Violet has been trying to think of some theories that might be helpful for friend-making, and so far her best idea is called the Theory of Swapping Small Things. The theory is that if two people give each other a small thing, they might end up becoming very good friends. She had the idea because Mama and Vincent got married in their old garden and when they said "I do," they gave each other small gold rings, which they both wear all the time. It was a good swap, Violet thinks, since now they are very special friends. They laugh and smile almost all the time when they are together, and Vincent brings Mama a flower nearly every day. Violet doesn't have a spare ring, but she does have a few special small things that she could try swapping with the girl next door. Perhaps one of them would be perfect.

She squats down and puts her eye close to the hole, spying through it like a telescope. The garden she sees is very different from her own, which is messy with lots of weeds and long grass because no one has had time to do any proper gardening yet. In the neighbors' garden there is no mess. There isn't a single weed or a slightly overgrown patch. It is the neatest, tidiest garden Violet has ever seen. It has a soft, green lawn

trimmed very short, with hedges clipped into special squarish shapes. The owners must be very neat, tidy people, Violet thinks.

Then she has a slightly worrying thought. A family of tidy people might not be very pleased to discover a small hole in their fence.

Only a minute ago Violet had been trying to think of a good small thing to swap with the girl next door. But now she is not thinking at all about making a new friend or testing her new theory. She is thinking about the tidy neighbors knocking crossly on the door and saying, "Why is there a hole in our fence, and who put it there?" That is a *very* worrying thought.

When it gets close to bedtime, Violet is still worrying. She would like to tell Mama and Vincent about the hole before the neighbors come over. Mama and Vincent might be cross too, but they might also have some useful ideas. Vincent might say that they could fill the hole with the stuff he has been using to fix the bathroom cracks. Mama might say that they could make a special ginger cake with lemon icing that says, "Sorry about the hole in your fence."

But everybody looks tired after a day of moving into the new house. They do not look as if they are in the mood to fill holes or make cakes. They are flopping on the couch and chairs, which aren't in quite the right spots yet, and watching the one channel Nicola has managed to find on the new television. So Violet does not tell anybody about her worrying thought.

Something she particularly likes about the new house is that now she has her own bunk bed. Violet slept in a bunk bed once at a beach house and has wanted one ever since. She sleeps in the bottom bunk with a sheet draped down so it makes a small personal space. It is a good place for thinking, even if the thinking is mostly worrying, which it is tonight. But before she goes to sleep, Violet has an idea about the problem of the hole in the fence.

2
The Silver Bell

Sometimes when you wake up in the morning and think about an idea you had the night before, it doesn't seem quite as good. At other times it seems even better than it did when you first thought of it. Violet's idea about the hole in the fence is the second sort.

Before she has had breakfast or even has said hello to anyone, Violet looks through her Box of Small Things and takes out a tiny silver bell. It is the kind that dangles on the bottom of a skirt from India, and if there are lots, they jingle. Violet has only one bell so it does not quite jingle, but she likes it and has been saving it for something important. She wraps it up in a small piece of purple tissue paper saved from a present Vincent once gave her. Then she sticks it together with a sliver of sticky tape. It is the smallest present she has ever wrapped.

Next, Violet writes a message on a piece of paper not much bigger than a postage stamp, using her tiniest, tiniest handwriting. She writes:

Hello, I'm sorry I made a hole in the fence. It was an accident. I hope you are not cross. Here is a present for you. Love from Violet

Then she draws a tiny violet and folds up the note. It is the smallest note she has ever written.

Violet takes the present and the note out to the garden and puts them into the hole in the fence. They rest perfectly in the curve of the wood. Her idea is that if a person notices something like a hole in their fence, they would probably go over and look at it closely. And if they find an apologizing note and a small present waiting there, perhaps they are less likely to mind too much. It is a good idea, Violet thinks.

When everybody else gets up, there are lots of things to do. Dylan has a violin exam in the afternoon, so he is practicing nearly every minute, and it is Violet's job to turn the pages of the music book for him. Dylan cannot talk at the same time as he plays the violin, not even just to say, "Turn the page now, please." So he wrinkles his nose when it is time for

Violet to turn the page. Violet listens to the music, watches Dylan's nose very carefully, and thinks and thinks about the present in the hole in the fence.

Mama has been knitting owls for a friend's shop, and the owls have to be finished by the afternoon, but they don't have eyes yet, because she has been so busy unpacking. So Violet helps with the eyes, and then in the afternoon she and Mama deliver the owls together. It is a shop Violet likes and usually she is glad when Mama stops for a chat with her friend because that means there is time to look around.

But this afternoon Violet is thinking nonstop about the tidy neighbors and wonders if they have noticed the hole or found the note and the silver bell. So although there are a lot of new and interesting things at the shop—like crocheted cupcakes and doughnuts, and notebooks with felt ladybugs on the covers, which Violet especially likes—most of all she just wants to go home.

As soon as they get back, Violet runs out to the garden. She can see from a few steps away that there is still a tiny tissue-wrapped present and note in the hole. She is slightly relieved because it means that the tidy neighbors probably haven't noticed. But she is also a bit disappointed because it would have been nice for them to find the silver bell and not be cross.

However, when she gets closer to the fence and looks more carefully, Violet notices something very interesting. The tissue parcel in the hole is not purple anymore. It is *pink*.

3 The Pink Parcel

Violet takes the pink-tissue parcel out of the hole. There is also a tiny note. Mama says it is polite to open cards before presents, but as far as Violet knows there are no rules about notes and, anyway, no one is there to be polite for. So she unwraps the pink parcel first, very carefully peeling away a tiny piece of sticky tape.

Inside the parcel is a beautiful tiny purple gemstone. It is about the size of Violet's little fingernail. She knows the proper name for it because Nicola has some precious gemstone beads and a book that tells you which stones are which. Nicola has shown the book to Violet, so Violet knows that the icy purple ones are called amethysts. They are her favorite of all the gemstones. It is a very good present, she thinks.

Next she unfolds the tiny note.
The handwriting is a little bit like
hers but neater. It says:

Hello Violet,
Thank you for the lovely bell. Don't
worry about the hole. I am not cross
and no one else has noticed except me.
Here is a present for you too.
Would you like to come over tomorrow
morning?
Love from Rose

At the bottom of the note is a
tiny drawing of a rose.

Violet folds the note up, wraps the amethyst back in the pink tissue, and puts them both in her pocket. But she keeps taking them out and looking at them again and again.

Even though Violet does not want to tell anyone the secret of the hole in the fence, she does tell Mama about Rose's invitation. (If you don't mention where an invitation comes from, even a strangely small one, people usually don't ask you any questions about it.) Mama says she

can go, so Violet puts another note
in the hole that says *Yes, please*
signed with a violet. Later on, Mama
knocks on the new neighbors' door
to see what time Violet should come
and also to borrow a can opener,
since the Mackerels' can opener is
still in a box somewhere and no one
can find it.

Violet does not go with Mama,
because she wants to do some
planning before she meets Rose
for the first time. Since they have

swapped small things, perhaps they will become very good friends. And on the day you meet a very good friend for the first time, Violet thinks it might be important to wear something special.

In her new room there is a box of old clothes that Nicola has out-grown. Mama says most of them will still be a bit big for Violet, but Violet has been having seconds of dinner quite a lot lately, and she might be bigger than people think. In the box she finds a skirt that used to be Nicola's favorite. It is dark purple, and when Nicola twirled very fast, it flew out into a perfect fluttering circle. Violet tries the skirt on. She breathes out as much as she can, but the skirt is still a bit loose. Then she has the idea of pegging it at the side with a wooden clothes peg. She twirls and it flies out perfectly.

Violet has a red-and-white stripy top that is long enough to cover the peg. She tries it on and looks in the mirror on the inside of her wardrobe door. All you can see of the peg is a slight lump at the side. It is a good outfit for meeting a possible very good friend for the first time, Violet thinks.

She lays it all out on her chair, ready for tomorrow, and puts the small amethyst in the pocket of the stripy top. Then

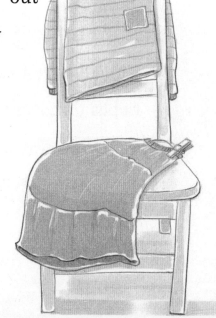

she puts her pajamas on and wishes
and wishes that the morning would
hurry up.

Before she goes to bed, she checks
the hole in the fence one more time.
There is a new note there. It says

See you tomorrow!

signed with a rose. Violet hopes and
hopes that Rose might turn out to be
a very good friend.

4 The Missing Sock

Violet wakes up so early the next morning that it is still a bit dark outside. She gets dressed straight-away in her skirt and top. She wishes she could find both of her favorite purple socks instead of only one purple sock and a red sock. But when she puts her boots on, you can hardly tell that they are different. Mama and Vincent like people to wait until it is completely light, and preferably even a big longer, before going into their room and asking them to do things like look for lost socks. So Violet chooses some books from the pile Mama unpacked yesterday and waits for the sun to rise properly.

When the sun is finally all the way up and there are shuffling noises and the sound of the kettle on in the kitchen, Violet runs downstairs. After breakfast, she takes some muffins that she and Vincent made and places them very carefully into a box to take to Rose's house.

At last, it is time to go next door. Mama comes too, to return the borrowed can opener. Violet is glad, because even when you have really been looking forward to meeting someone for the first time, you can get slight butterflies when it actually happens. It is nice if someone goes with you, at least as far as the door.

Violet rings the doorbell, and Rose's mama answers. A lovely smell of perfume wafts out onto the porch. Rose's mama has on red lipstick and is wearing a perfectly white shirt without any wrinkles, like someone on television. Violet suspects Mama's shirt was once white too, but now it is a lot of different colors. It is the one she wears to do things like painting and unpacking boxes, so there are also quite a few wrinkles.

While Mama gives back the can

opener, and they say for quite a long time what a nice community it is and how handy to have a fruit and vegetable market just around the corner, Violet stands behind Mama and peeps in. Sometimes she peeps at exactly the same moment as the girl who is standing behind Rose's mama peeps too. She is wearing a perfectly white dress, like a girl in a magazine. When they catch each other peeping a few times in a row, they both get the giggles. After that, when Rose's mama says, "Rose, why don't you take Violet upstairs and show her your room?" Rose says, "Come in, Violet!" and Violet runs inside as if they are already very good friends.

Although Rose is jiggling a little bit and doing an excited sort of squeak, her dress stays as unwrinkly as her mama's shirt. She even has matching white hair clips. Violet puts her hand over her peg lump.

"We take our shoes off indoors,"

says Rose quickly. "It's so the carpet doesn't get ruined."

Violet takes her boots off and puts them beside a neat row of shoes near the door. She wishes very much that she had been able to find her other favorite sock, or, in fact, any two socks that were the same. Rose's socks match perfectly, and they are white with a pink rose on each ankle. Violet does

a little swallow and follows Rose up

the soft, carpeted stairs to her room.

5
The Dollhouse

Violet has never been in a room like Rose's before. Everything is pink or white or both, and her bed has a floaty curtain all around it called a canopy. There is an oval mirror on a stand that tilts backward and forward, and a dresser with pink crystal

knobs. And beside the dresser on a pink rug is the loveliest dollhouse Violet has ever, ever seen. Rose wants to show her lots of other beautiful things, but Violet cannot stop looking at the dollhouse.

Rose doesn't seem to mind. "Want to see inside?" she asks.

"Yes, please!" says Violet.

Rose pulls out the dollhouse and a box of dolls and furniture. Violet tucks her differently socked feet underneath her and looks, not daring to touch. There is a tiny grand piano, a lampshade, an oven with pots and pans, a bath with gold taps, a sofa, a dining table with chairs, and even a cheese platter with cheeses and a silver knife.

"Do you have a dollhouse?" asks Rose.

Violet does have one that she and Nicola made in a shoe box. They made a chest of drawers by sticking matchboxes together and gluing on beads for knobs, and they made a mirror by covering a tiddlywink in silver foil. Even though she does have a sort of dollhouse, Violet says, "Not really," quite softly. The shoe-box sort probably doesn't count, she suspects.

"How about you set up the living room?" asks Rose. "And I'll set up the bedroom."

Violet likes choosing the pieces of furniture from the box and deciding where they should go. Rose sets up a tiny canopy bed, a pink rug, and a little tilting mirror on a stand.

"That looks just like your bedroom!" says Violet.

"I know," says Rose. "I've been collecting the pieces for ages. I wish there was a dresser like mine, though." Rose puts a little plain white one in the dollhouse bedroom. "They don't make them with pink crystal knobs."

Violet decorates the living room with a grandfather clock and some bookshelves with books on them. Rose does her excited squeak when she sees how it all looks. It is so much fun working on the dollhouse with Rose that Violet forgets to worry about her socks. When she kneels right down to look through the doorway into the kitchen, she forgets to worry about her peg, too.

"Why do you have a peg on your skirt?" asks Rose.

Violet pulls her stripy top back down as far as it will go.

"It's my sister's old skirt and it's still a bit big for me," she says,

wishing and wishing that she had a
perfect dress like Rose's.

"That's a clever idea," says Rose.
She looks thoughtfully at the peg
lump.

Violet and Rose have their
morning tea, sitting on special high
stools beside the kitchen counter.

There is a fresh pine for-esty smell and a nice soft hum coming from the dishwasher. The only thing on the shiny kitchen counter is a bro-chure from a bakery, open to some pink and white cupcakes with sugar flowers on top. Violet thinks about the box of muffins she and Vincent made and wonders if Rose normally has iced cupcakes with flowers for morning tea.

"Mama is ordering those for my birthday party," says Rose.

"They're beautiful," says Violet. She would like to taste one, but she suspects Rose probably doesn't invite peg-wearers to her parties.

Rose's mama pours their juice into tall glasses and adds ice cubes from a special box in the freezer, using tongs. Violet watches carefully. She has never had ice from tongs before, and some-how it seems nicer than ordinary ice. The muffins Violet brought look very plain next to the cupcakes in the picture, even though Violet chose the best ones to bring. But Rose and her mama both eat two and say they are delicious.

After morning tea they go back to the dollhouse, and Violet has the idea of taking the small amethyst out of her pocket and putting it on the table as a centerpiece. That gives Rose the idea of taking the tiny silver bell out of her treasure pouch and hanging it on the door as a doorbell. Rose squeaks and Violet does a small squeak too, just to see what it feels like.

Later on, when Mama knocks on the real door and says it is time for Violet to come home, instead of packing up the dollhouse, Rose says they should slide it carefully back beside the dresser as it is, so they can keep working on it another day. The only things they change are the amethyst, which goes back into

Violet's pocket, and the silver bell, which goes back into Rose's treasure pouch.

Violet smiles, even though it is time to leave and she would much rather stay. The Theory of Swapping Small Things might be quite a good theory, she thinks. But as she puts her boots back on over her odd socks, she is still not sure.

6 The Potted-Plant Gecko

In the afternoon, after doing some more unpacking and organizing, Violet and Mama sit down for a cool drink, and Violet would like to put ice in hers. She looks in the new freezer in case there is a special icebox like Rose's, but there is only a normal tray of ice. Violet asks Mama if there are any little silver ice tongs in the boxes they haven't unpacked yet. Mama says not as far as she knows.

While they have their tray-ice drinks in ordinary glasses, Violet tells Mama about Rose's lovely tall glasses, the special no-shoes carpet, the shiny kitchen counter, and the flowery cupcakes Rose is having at her party. Mama says, "How lovely," but she says it in a slightly tired way. Violet tells her about Rose's crystal-knob dresser, the pine forest smell, and the nice hum of the dishwasher. Mama seems to look even more exhausted than when she first sat down.

Just as Violet is asking if Mama
would like to hear about the special
liquid soap she saw in Rose's bathroom, Vincent comes in and says, "I
bet Rose doesn't have a gecko in her

potted plant," and they all go out onto the back porch to see the tiny lizard he has found. It has a nice friendly face and small suckers on its feet. She wonders if Rose would be interested in seeing a lizard so tiny that it could easily fit in your pocket.

As she thinks about it, she puts her hand in her pocket and her fingers twiddle the small piece of amethyst Rose gave her. If Rose liked the gecko, she might also like some of the other interesting things Violet has found at the new house, like the ants' nest and the ring of little umbrella mushrooms. She might even like to see Violet's new room and her bunk bed. So Violet asks Mama and Vincent if she can invite Rose over, and they say yes.

Violet writes a small note asking if Rose would like to come over. Rose will be her first guest at the new house and that is quite special, so she draws some stars around the message before putting the note in the hole in the fence. But as she goes back through the garden to her house, Violet thinks again of how messy it is compared with Rose's beautiful, neat garden.

Violet's room is not pink and white, and her things do not match like Rose's. They are all different, and maybe Rose won't think that is quite as nice. There will be only normal ice and ordinary soap for Rose to use. And another worrying thought is the dollhouse. Violet wonders what Rose will think about being very good friends with a person who has a dollhouse that is only the shoe-box sort.

Violet twiddles the amethyst and thinks of the gecko, and there are some hopeful thoughts in among her worrying ones.

Very soon the note disappears, and Violet finds another one saying:

7
The Party Invitation

The next day, when there is finally a knock at the door, Violet runs down to answer it. Violet says that Rose doesn't have to take off her shoes, because the carpet is not the special sort, and Rose looks pleased. Even though Violet feels a bit shy about showing Rose around a house that smells more like toast and honey than a fresh pine forest, it is fun giving her a tour because Rose is so curious about everything and does her excited squeak lots of times.

Rose is interested in all the things Violet points out, like the ring of mushrooms, the ants' nest in the garden, and the Indian curtains Mama is hanging up that Vincent brought back from Mumbai. But she is also very interested in things that Violet herself hardly notices, like the yogurt Vincent is making in a jar in the kitchen. It's just what Violet has for breakfast every morning, so she had not thought of showing it to Rose. But Rose has never seen anyone make yogurt before and asks Vincent lots of questions.

Rose is very interested in Mama's knitting basket too. It is full of woolly toadstools she is making to go in the shop Violet likes. A few of them still need spots, and some don't even have their stuffing in yet.

"I can't believe your mama actually *makes* these," says Rose, picking up a toadstool as carefully as if it were a baby bird.

"She can knit owls and gnomes and fish, too," says Violet, "and also rabbits."

Best of all, Rose likes Violet's room. Violet shows her the blue china bird Vincent gave her, and the bridesmaid's dress with wings that Mama made for her out of a night-gown. They take Violet's Box of Small Things into the personal space in Violet's bunk bed, which Rose says is exactly like being in a real tent. Violet has never shared that space with anybody else before, but it is nice to sit there with Rose, especially when she spots a button shaped like

a tiny rose and does another of her

excited squeaks.

Later on, after Violet has shown

Rose how to make a Box of Small

Things and Rose has told Violet about

the kinds of things you can keep in a treasure pouch, Rose's mama knocks at the door and Vincent invites her in for a cup of tea. Rose's mama says it has been a long day and that would be very nice, so Mama makes a pot and Vincent puts out the rest of the leftover muffins.

Rose watches Mama spooning tea leaves into the teapot.

"Do we have tea leaves at our house, Mama, or just ordinary tea bags?" asks Rose.

"Just ordinary tea bags, I think," says Rose's mama.

"Did you know Violet and Vincent *made* these muffins?" Rose asks. "And they make yogurt, and Violet has it every day for breakfast!"

"How lovely," says Rose's mama in a slightly tired way.

"And Violet's mama makes all kinds of things, too," says Rose. "She can knit toadstools with spots, and owls and gnomes and fish. And she made Violet a bridesmaid's dress with wings!"

Rose's mama seems to look even more exhausted than when she first sat down.

Vincent suggests that Violet gets the gecko from the potted plant since it is becoming a bit more tame now and Rose hasn't seen it yet. Everyone looks at its friendly face and the little suckers on its feet. Rose would like to have a turn holding it, and she squeaks when Vincent puts it gently in her hands. The two mamas have more tea and talk for a long time.

That evening, a little while after Rose has gone home, Violet finds a note waiting for her in the hole in the fence. It looks more special than the other notes because it is on pink paper with sparkly edges, and instead of being folded, it is curled into a scroll. It says:

Dear Violet,
You are invited to my birthday party, on Saturday at 11:00. It is a flower party, so you can dress as any flower you'd like. I am going to be a rose, so maybe you can be a violet. Hope you can come. Love from Rose

Violet smiles and twiddles the piece of amethyst in her pocket.

8 The Matchbox Dresser

Violet is quite excited about the invitation. She has never been to a flower party before, and she thinks about possible violet costumes she could make. She has a few good ideas. But then she has a very different kind of thought. What if Rose and her guests all have the sorts of costumes you get from an actual costume shop? What if they all look like real flowers and Violet is the only one at the party wearing green tights and a purple, pegged, hand-me-down skirt? Suddenly Violet's mind fills up with worries again.

After she has worried for a while about her costume, Violet starts worrying about what sort of birthday present she will give to Rose. Usually Mama or Nicola help her make birthday presents for people's parties, like a peg doll or a beaded bookmark or a library bag with the person's name sewn on it. Even though Violet thinks those are all very good presents, she can't imagine any of them being in Rose's beautiful room. Perhaps other guests at the party will bring big presents that will all be pink and white. And Violet might have only a small present to bring, which might not be pink *or* white. That is a *very* worrying thought.

"You're very quiet this evening, Violet," says Vincent at dinnertime. Everyone has been talking about plans for the new garden, and Violet has not been talking about anything at all. "Is something the matter?"

"No," says Violet. Her voice

sounds a bit cross, even though she doesn't really feel it. When your mind is full of worrying thoughts, it can be difficult to talk about ordinary things like whether or not there should be a barbecue and a special outdoor table and chairs, and sometimes that can make your voice sound cross.

Later on, at bedtime, while Mama is tucking her in, she asks, "Are you sure nothing is wrong, Violet? You don't seem like yourself tonight."

"I seem *exactly* like myself to me," says Violet. She sounds cross again, even though she still isn't really. "I just have some worrying thoughts, that's all."

"Sometimes worries don't seem

as bad if you tell someone about them," says Mama.

"Unless they say, 'That is a silly thing to worry about,'" points out Violet.

"What if I promise not to say that?" suggests Mama.

So Violet tells Mama about the problems of the costume and the present.

Mama thinks for a little while.

"A good way of making yourself feel worried is by thinking about what you don't have and can't do," she says, "but a good trick for feeling better again is by thinking about what you *do* have and *can* do."

Violet wishes very, very much that she had a perfect violet costume and a present for Rose that was as big and beautiful as the dollhouse. But as she goes to sleep, she tries Mama's trick.

And in the morning Violet has an idea. She looks around the house for empty matchboxes. Vincent has some in his old camping kit, and he doesn't mind tipping the matches from the nearly empty boxes into the nearly full boxes, so he gives Violet three empty matchboxes. Nicola keeps her jewelry-making supplies in matchboxes so she has a small collection and gives Violet another two. And Violet

herself has one in her Box of Small Things. Six is enough, she thinks.

She glues the matchboxes in two stacks of three and glues a piece of stiff white card across the top, like the surface of a dresser. Then she cuts off a strip of some beautiful white pearly paper from a wedding invitation. Violet has been saving it for something special. She wraps it around the sides of the boxes and glues it in place. It is a very good mini dresser, but it does look a bit like the plain white one that Rose already has. That is because Violet has not finished yet.

In Nicola's book about gemstones, Violet's second favorite stone after the amethyst is an icy pink gem, called the rose quartz. Nicola has some rose quartz beads in one of her matchboxes, and Violet hopes Nicola might give her six very small ones.

It is a good time to ask Nicola for things because her room in the new house is bigger than her old one, and she is very happy about it. People often say yes to things when they are already feeling happy. So although the beads are quite precious, Nicola doesn't mind giving six to Violet. She also lends Violet her special glue that dries quickly. With the pink crystal knobs on the drawers, the dresser looks almost like Rose's real one. Not exactly, but almost.

When the dresser is finished, Violet shows it to Vincent. He looks closely and opens the drawers very carefully by their rose quartz knobs.

"Do you think it's a good enough present for Rose?" Violet asks him.

"I think it's a good enough present for anybody," says Vincent.

"Not all people like homemade presents," says Violet, worrying again.

"But some people like that sort of present the best," says Vincent. "I do."

Violet hopes and hopes that Rose does too.

Next, Violet asks Nicola about the flower costume, hoping she is happy enough about her new room to help with two worries. Nicola thinks the purple skirt is just right, and she has a green top she can lend Violet that is only slightly too big and will hide the peg completely. Violet eventually finds her other purple sock in one of Mama's boxes. When she tries it all on, she does look a bit like an upside-down violet.

Nicola also has another idea. Violet once helped her to cut out felt leaves as part of a school project, and Nicola thinks they could make some similar leaves for Violet's costume. They cut heart-shaped violet leaves out of green felt and stick them onto hairpins. When the glue has dried and Nicola puts the pins in Violet's hair, she looks almost exactly like an upside-down flower. Finally Nicola puts one of her own clear quartz necklaces around Violet's neck. The small, watery beads look like morning dewdrops on violet petals.

"Do you think this will be all right to wear to Rose's party?"

Violet asks Nicola. "The others will probably have perfect costumes from a shop."

"I think it will be fine," says Nicola.

Violet hopes that Nicola is right.

There is just enough felt left to cut out three small, jagged rose-leaf shapes to put on hairpins so Rose can have leaves in her hair too, if she likes. They fit perfectly in the drawers of the matchbox chest.

For Rose's birthday card, Violet

draws a violet and a rose. She looks at the card and twiddles the amethyst in her pocket. Then she draws a ribbon tied in a bow around the two flowers. She hopes and hopes that Rose will like it.

Mostly, though, Violet is hoping she will not be the only person at the party whose costume is not from a shop. Also she hopes at least one other person at the party will have only a small present for Rose.

9 The Birthday Party

On the morning of the party, Violet's hopes seem to fade away, like a small splash of water on a very hot day. She puts the matchbox dresser right at the back of her cupboard with the shoe-box dollhouse. She puts the violet costume away with her very ordinary clothes. And at breakfast, when Mama suggests a big bowl of muesli and yogurt to give her extra energy for the party, Violet says quietly, "I'm not going to the party."

"Then what will you do with that clever matchbox dresser you made?" asks Vincent.

"Nothing," says Violet. And it is a sad thought because she worked very hard on it.

"You might not get the chance to wear that beautiful violet costume again for a long time," says Nicola. "Not very many people have flower parties."

"I don't mind," says Violet.

But actually, it is another sad thought. Violet has never heard of anyone besides Rose having a flower party.

"Did you make Rose a card?" asks Dylan. He is very good at drawing, and he likes looking at other people's drawings.

Violet is too sad to eat even a very small bowl of muesli and yogurt, so she goes upstairs to get the card she made to show Dylan.

"A violet and a rose," says Dylan. "And you actually made the ribbon curl around like real ribbon does!"

Mama comes around to look at the curling ribbon.

"What a beautiful card," she says. "I think Rose would love it."

"Really?" asks Violet.

"Really," says Mama.

"Well, maybe I'll go for a little while, just to see what it's like," says Violet.

She puts on her costume and wraps up the matchbox dresser, with the leaf hair clips tucked inside. Mama gives her some pink rosy ribbon to tie the parcel with, which curls to match the card. And then it is time to go.

Violet takes a deep breath. Standing on the doorstep, she can hear lots of voices inside Rose's house. Rose's mama answers the door, dressed up as a hibiscus flower with a red dress and a sort of yellow crown for the stalky part in the middle. It is a very, very beautiful costume and definitely the kind that comes from a fancy costume shop. Violet does a little swallow.

Violet follows her inside and straightaway sees another grown-up with a very beautiful costume. It is a daisy dress with a bright yellow bodice, a stiff white petal tutu, and white petal wings on the back. There are little green silk slippers, which must be all right on the special carpet, Violet thinks, because the daisy is wearing them inside. Her face is painted with tiny sparkling daisies. Violet does a big swallow and looks down at her purple woolly socks. She wonders if it is too late to run back home.

"Hello, Violet!" squeaks Rose.

"This is the flower-fairy face painter for my party!"

The daisy, whose actual name is Simone, has a little suitcase full of paints, brushes, and glitter. She is trying to paint a sparkly rose on Rose's cheek with a tiny paintbrush, and she is laughing and asking Rose to keep her face still. But Rose can't, because she keeps wanting to smile at Violet. That makes Violet feel better, but only a bit.

A daffodil, a tulip, a fuchsia, and

a lily are crowding around, waiting for their turn, and while they all wait and watch, a dandelion and a forget-me-not arrive and crowd around too. The daffodil has a headdress with big yellow petals blooming out all round her face, and the fuchsia looks like a ballerina with a pink and purple petal dress and red tights so her legs look like the dangly parts. Rose herself has a swirly pink silk skirt that looks as soft as real rose petals.

But there are some other costumes too. A slightly gloomy-looking boy in a green tracksuit is supposed to be a cornflower, but he doesn't want to wear his blue hat, so he is just a stalk. One girl has an antennae headband and a skirt with black spots. She says she doesn't have a flower costume, so she has come as a ladybug, and someone giggles.

"Ladybugs live in flowers," says Violet, who knows quite a bit about ladybugs. "I think it's a good costume for a flower party."

The ladybug smiles and lets Violet try on her antennae while Simone paints a sparkly bug on the ladybug's face.

Soon it is Violet's turn to have her face painted. While she is keeping still so her violet doesn't get smudged, she watches other people giving Rose their presents. The daffodil gives her a matching jewelry set with a locket, a

ring, and some earrings for pierced ears, even though Rose doesn't have pierced ears yet. Rose squeaks happily. The forget-me-not gives her a nail-polish kit and a little electric fan for drying your nails. Rose squeaks even more. Violet looks sadly at her small present. Rose will not squeak when she opens it. Violet does not want to give it to her at all. So when no one is looking, she hides it behind a vase.

Her only hope now is that there are so many big presents from her very good friends that Rose might not notice if there is none from just an ordinary friend. No present is probably better than a dresser made of matchboxes, Violet thinks.

Next, Simone says it is time for some games. She shows everyone a game where she puts lots of flowers on a tray and then covers them all up and you have to remember as many of the different kinds as you can. They play other games too, and people win glittery pens and flower bangles. Even though Violet is feeling quite sad, she wins a notebook for pinning the poppy on the stem with a blindfold on. The stalk looks gloomy again after winning hair clips in a round of pass the parcel, so Violet gives him her notebook. She suspects you shouldn't really win a prize if you don't give a present. The stalk looks a bit less gloomy after that.

Then they have the birthday cupcakes, which look even more beautiful than they did in the brochure, with sparklers and candles burning between them for Rose to blow out while everyone sings "Happy Birthday to You."

After the cakes, everyone goes outside into Rose's beautiful garden to play a game where you have to stand back and throw a wishing pebble into the sunflower. If it lands in the petals, you get to keep the pebble, and if it lands in the middle, Simone gives you a much more special pebble with a flower painted on it. It is a good game, Violet thinks, and she would like to win a pebble. But much more than that, she would like to go home.

Violet goes over to Rose and taps her on the shoulder, to tell the small fib of a slight headache and to say an early good-bye. But before she can say anything, Rose squeaks and whispers something in her ear.

10

The Thank-You Note

"Come inside for a minute. I want to show you something," whispers Rose.

Everybody is busy, so no one notices them disappearing into the house and up the stairs together. Violet wonders if Rose now has a whole *street* of pink and white dollhouses to show her. On the way, Violet grabs her present from behind the vase. If you only have a small thing to give someone, it can be easier without everyone watching.

There are a few new birthday things in Rose's room. There are white cushions on her canopy bed that spell out "R-O-S-E" in pink letters, and there is a shiny new car beside the dollhouse. But those are not what Rose wants to show Violet.

"Look!" says Rose, pulling up her green top, which has leafy points all around the collar, to show Violet the top of her beautiful swirly rose-pink skirt. At the side there is a wooden peg.

"It's my mama's skirt," says Rose. "She said we could get it made the right size for the party, but I wanted a peg, so it would be like yours."

Violet pulls up her green top to show her matching peg. It is a funny surprise but a very nice one. They both twirl, and their skirts fly out in fluttering circles.

"I wish I had leaves in my hair,"

says Rose, admiring Violet's. "Then we would *really* match."

Violet takes a deep breath and holds out her present.

"It's only very small," she says.

Rose opens the card Violet made.

"A rose and a violet! That's us!" she says.

Then she carefully unwraps the present. Suddenly her eyes get very big.

"It's my dresser!" she squeaks. She holds it up to compare it with her own actual dresser. "It's perfect!" she squeaks again and does some slight twirling.

Violet is so happy she wants to squeak and twirl too.

Rose pulls out the dollhouse to put it in the bedroom right away, but Violet says, "Look inside the drawers first."

Pulling open the drawers with the tiny rose quartz knobs, Rose takes out the little jagged leaf hair clips and squeaks even more. Violet puts them in Rose's hair, and they look at themselves in her special tilting mirror. They are a matching leafy rose and violet. Rose gives Violet a thank-you hug,

and they put the matchbox dresser in the dollhouse. It is a very good fit. Then they run back downstairs. No one has even noticed they were missing.

After that, it feels like almost no time before the parents start arriving to pick everyone up and the party is over. Violet says good-bye to the ladybug and the stalk and thank you to Simone and Rose's mama. Rose says good-bye and thank you to most of the guests as they leave, but when Violet leaves she gives her another big hug. No one needs to pick Violet up because she only has to walk back next door.

"Did you have a good time?" asks Mama later on, while Violet is in the bath carefully washing around the sparkly violet on her cheek.

"I had a very good time," says Violet.

That evening, in the hole in the fence, she finds a note from Rose saying thank you again for the dresser and the hair clips. It is addressed to MY VERY GOOD FRIEND VIOLET, and at the bottom is a picture of a violet and a rose, tied together with a ribbon. Violet twiddles the piece of amethyst in her pocket. The Theory of Swapping Small Things might be quite a good theory, she thinks.